For all who practice kindness.
(Sometimes it takes lots of practice.)
And especially for Colby,
Ella, and Gretchen.

SIMON & SCHUSTER BOOKS FOR YOUNG READERS
An imprint of Simon & Schuster Children's Publishing Division
1230 Avenue of the Americas, New York, New York 10020
Copyright © 2020 by Apryl Stott
SIMON & SCHUSTER BOOKS FOR YOUNG READERS is a trademark of Simon & Schuster, Inc.
For information about special discounts for bulk purchases, please contact
Simon & Schuster Special Sales at 1-866-506-1949 or business@simonandschuster.com.
The Simon & Schuster Speakers Bureau can bring authors to your live event.
For more information or to book an event, contact the Simon & Schuster Speakers Bureau
at 1-866-248-3049 or visit our website at www.simonspeakers.com.
Book design by Chloë Foglia
The text for this book was set in Horley Old Style.
The illustrations for this book were rendered in watercolor paint and digital ink.
Manufactured in the United States of America
1020 LSC
4 6 8 10 9 7 5 3
Library of Congress Cataloging-in-Publication Data
Names: Stott, Apryl, author, illustrator.
Title: Share some kindness, bring some light / Apryl Stott.
Description: First edition. | New York : Simon & Schuster Books for Young Readers, [2020] | Audience: Ages 4–8. |
Audience: Grades 2–3. | Summary: Coco sets out to help her new friend, Bear, show other animals he is not mean just
because he is big, and soon they all have learned something about kindness.
Identifiers: LCCN 2019028334 (print) | LCCN 2019028335 (eBook) |
ISBN 9781534462380 (hardback) | ISBN 9781534462397 (eBook)
Subjects: CYAC: Kindness—Fiction. | Bears—Fiction. | Animals—Fiction.
Classification: LCC PZ7.1.S759 Sh 2020 (print) | LCC PZ7.1.S759 (eBook) | DDC [E]—dc23
LC record available at https://lccn.loc.gov/2019028334
LC eBook record available at https://lccn.loc.gov/2019028335

Share Some Kindness, Bring Some Light

APRYL STOTT

Simon & Schuster Books for Young Readers
NEW YORK LONDON TORONTO SYDNEY NEW DELHI

Coco and Bear were friends from almost the first time they met. They were very different: Bear was big. Coco was small. Bear was shy. Coco was brave.

But they were exactly alike in the most important way.

"I like that you're kind," said Coco.

"That's my favorite thing about you, too," said Bear.

"I also like that you're such a good dancer," said Coco.

"I wish the animals knew all the good things that you know about me," sighed Bear.

"They don't?" asked Coco.

"They say that I must be mean,
'cause I'm so big. And some of
them are afraid of me."

"Noodle strudel," said Coco
in disbelief.
"Yeah," said Bear, sniffling.

Coco gave Bear a big, tight hug. Because that's what made
her feel better whenever she was sad.

After Bear got some of his sadness out,
Coco said, "My grandma always says:

WHEN LIFE GETS DARK
AS WINTER'S NIGHT,
SHARE SOME KINDNESS,
Bring Some Light.

If we can do that, maybe the
other animals will see what a
good, kind Bear you are."
"But how do you share kindness?"
asked Bear.

Coco thought a moment. "I think kindness must be something that you can give away. Like a gift."
"We can bake cookies to share," suggested Bear.
"Yeah!" agreed Coco.

"But how do we bring light?" asked Bear.
"Let's make lanterns," said Coco. "They're so cozy!"
"I have supplies in my cave that we can use," offered Bear.

When they were finished, they loaded up Bear's sled with all their gifts.

"Ready?" asked Coco.

Bear nodded. "Ready!" But then he whispered, "And a little scared. . . ."

"It's okay to be scared," said Coco. "So long as you don't let the scariness stop you from sharing kindness and bringing light."

Their first stop was Badger's house.

Badger was not impressed.
"I only eat cookies with worms in them," he said grumpily.
"Would you like a lantern instead?" asked Bear.

"How am I supposed to sleep all day with that
light in here?" said Badger. "No thank you!"

Next they tried Rabbit's house.

"Why would you bring me gifts?" asked Rabbit.

"We want to show you how kind my friend Bear is!" said Coco hopefully.

"What if you're trying to trick me? A big bear wouldn't want to be friends with a small rabbit like me. No thank you."

They didn't have much
luck with Hedgehog . . .

. . . or Skunk, either.

"I'm ready for a break," sighed Bear.

"Maybe we need to make some different gifts and try again tomorrow," said Coco.

The walk home was cold, and the only sound was the crunch of paws and boots through snow. Until . . .

"Heeeeelp!"

"Did you hear that?" asked Bear.

"It's coming from over there!" said Coco, pointing. She leaped off the path and . . .

FLOOMP!

"Quick! Climb on my back!" said Bear.

"Heeeeelp!" came the cry again.

"Why, it's Baby Deer!" said Coco. "What are you doing way out here?" she asked.
"I went on an adventure," said Baby Deer, shivering.
"Oh, we love adventures," said Bear.
"I do too," said Baby Deer. "But now I'm stuck!"

"Don't be afraid," said Coco. "We can help you!"
"How?" asked Baby Deer.
"You can ride on my back too," said Bear.

"Baby Deer! Baby Deer! Where are you?"
the animals cried as they searched.

"Here I am!" shouted Baby Deer. "I got stuck in the snow,
but Coco and Bear found me! They gave me a ride home."

"Oh, thank you!" said Mama Deer.

"Wow, good thing Bear is so big!" exclaimed Rabbit.

"And brave," said Hedgehog.

"And friendly," added Skunk.

"I guess he *is* a kind bear," grumbled Badger.

"Bear! Did you hear that? They finally figured out that you're kind!" exclaimed Coco.

"But I don't understand," said Bear. "They didn't want our cookies or lanterns!"

"Your lanterns came in handy after all, but helping Baby Deer
showed how kind you really are," explained Mama Deer.
"But we just helped because it was the right thing to do," said Coco.
"Exactly," said Mama Deer.

"I guess kindness is about giving away love instead of gifts,"
said Bear. "It's doing something nice without expecting to get
anything in return."

Coco looked up at the stars. "I think I get it now."
"Get what?" asked Bear.
"When life gets dark as winter's night, share some kindness,
bring some light."

Coco grinned and started tapping her foot.
"But, Bear, there's one more thing that the
others still don't know about you."